Mom, put your hat on!

A Story About a Mom with Cancer

Written by Edie Anderson

Illustrated by Henrique C. Rampazzo

ISBN 978-1-64719-683-7

Printed on acid free paper.

This book is dedicated to my four beautiful children. They did not ask for their mom to get cancer but they handled it like champions. I am grateful for each one of them.

Thank you, Carter, Caden, Cienna, and Chloe for making me the happiest mom in the world.

You are the reason I fought so hard.

I remember when I was happy. My mom would play with me and my brother and sisters, and everything was fine. Outside was our most favorite place to be. We would run and play and have so much fun.

The sun was very shiny then. It was so shiny that I had to wear sunglasses. We would play at the pool and splash each other. Everything was perfect.

Then one night while I was asleep, my mom went to the emergency room at the hospital. Dad gathered us all around and told us, "Mom has cancer." I didn't know what that was, but I knew it was bad because Dad had a worried look on his face. Then I started to worry too.

Dad told us that mom had to stay in the hospital for a few days. My sisters and brother and I didn't know what to do. We felt very afraid. Dad said it's normal to be scared, try not to worry, mom is strong, and she is a fighter. "A fighter?" I thought. "What is she fighting?"

The next day we got
in the car and drove to the hospital. It was strange to
see mom lying in a hospital bed. She smiled and put her arms out
to us. She hugged me so tight. I felt so many different feelings all at once.
I had never felt this way before, so I started to cry.

We met mom's doctor. He wore a white coat and used big words. He's called an Oncologist. He told us, "I am going to do everything I can to help your mom get better." I thought to myself, "He must be a superhero."

I asked the oncologist what cancer is. He explained that bad cells grow in your body, and when you have a lot of those bad cells, they can push away the good cells. I saw my friend get pushed at recess once. That made me sad.

Then before the oncologist left the hospital room, he told my mom, "You have been given a gift. You are one of the lucky ones who, from this day forward will cherish every moment you are alive."

I wondered what was inside the gift since he didn't give her anything to unwrap.

I asked my mom if I could climb into her hospital bed with her.

She said with a smile "Of course little buddy."

Then I leaned over and asked her if she was going to be ok. I tried to be strong when I asked her, but this made my mom cry again.

She whispered to me, "I will fight with everything I've got — don't you worry."

I wish I could've stayed there with her all night so she could hold me.

But dad told us it was time to go home. Hopefully mom would get to come home soon too. I like it when she calls me her "little buddy."

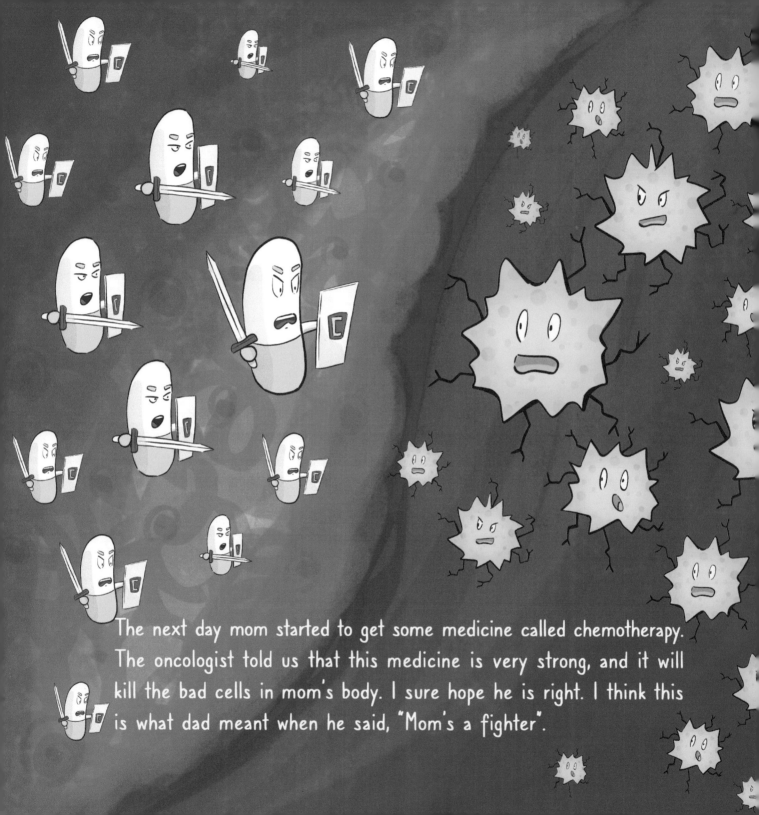

The next day mom started to get some medicine called chemotherapy. The oncologist told us that this medicine is very strong, and it will kill the bad cells in mom's body. I sure hope he is right. I think this is what dad meant when he said, "Mom's a fighter".

Things are very different now. Mom sleeps a lot. She is always sick and doesn't have enough energy to play with us. She also started to lose her hair. Dad said, "That's what happens when people with cancer get chemotherapy." I wish mom didn't lose her hair.

This was how it was for us. Mom was bald. She was fighting cancer and the sun wasn't very shiny anymore.

I asked my mom almost everyday "Why do you have cancer?" Sometimes I yelled and screamed because I was so mad that my mom had cancer and other moms didn't. I wish she would let ME fight her cancer. I would fight like a Tyrannosaurus Rex, because they are the meanest, strongest, most ferocious dinosaurs that ever lived.

One day when mom was driving us to school, I told her "Mom, put your hat on." She started to cry as she grabbed her hat and carefully put it on. I don't like that my mom doesn't have hair. I don't think she likes it either.

A little while later, dad told us that mom was going to have surgery. This is when a doctor takes out all the bad cells in her body. These bad cells connect and sometimes form a tumor. This is what happened inside my mom's body. The doctor is going to take out mom's tumor. This made me happy.

After the surgery, mom was very sore. She had to eat a special diet and needed help doing things like walking up the stairs, taking a shower, and other things that were pretty easy for me to do. Mom used to do these things by herself. Now she needs help.

So many people came to our house to help my mom. She has a lot of people who love her. Sometimes they brought me treats. I liked that.

I remember the day that the oncologist told my mom that she didn't need any more chemotherapy. The bad cells were all gone. Mom cried while smiling. I think parents do this a lot. Mom won the fight. She is the strongest person I know.

I was sad to know that not all moms win their fight like my mom did. For now, mom's bad cells are gone, and she has all good cells again. Everyday I tell those bad cells to stay away. I hope they never come back.

Now the sun is shiny again. Mom's hair is starting to grow back, so she doesn't have to wear a hat anymore. I can't wait for her hair to be just as long as it used to be. I am pretty sure mom wants it long again too.

I asked mom what the gift was that her oncologist gave her. She pulled me close, looked me right in the eyes and told me "Buddy, that gift was you. You and your brother and sisters are the reason why I am alive. And that is worth more than any gift in the whole world." That made me happy.

Printed in the USA
CPSIA information can be obtained
at www.ICGtesting.com
LVHW061642281223
767654LV00016B/113